D0460674

DAVIDE CALI

PiANO PiANO

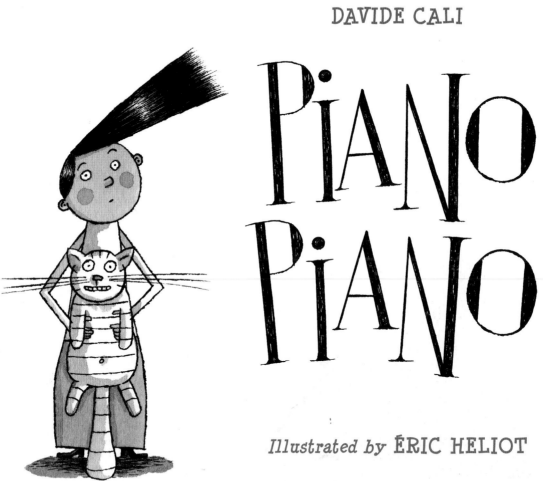

Illustrated by ÉRIC HELIOT

ini Charlesbridge

Every day at 3:00 sharp, Marcolino practices his scales.

Every day at 3:13, Marcolino
has had enough. He watches
his cartoons instead.

Every day at 3:14, Marcolino's mom asks, "What are you doing? Get back to the piano now!"

So Marcolino practices
his scales . . . again.

Every day at 3:18, he bangs his fists on the keyboard.

Marcolino's mom is always quick to remind him, "It's important to practice your scales! Without practice you won't become a grand pianist. When I was your age, I played for hours."

"Then why aren't *you* a grand pianist?"

"Because after you were born, I didn't have time to practice."

Marcolino feels bad that his mom never got
to be a grand pianist. So he returns to the piano
and plays . . . for her.

CLING
CLANG
CLONG

Every day it's the same thing,
except on Fridays.
That's when Marcolino's grandfather
takes him to the space museum.

But on this Friday, Grandpa asks, "Aren't you tired of visiting the same museum?"

"No. Besides, it's better than being at home."

"Why?"

"I don't want to be a grand pianist."

"So? Who says you have to be a grand pianist?"

"Mom. It's all my fault she didn't become a grand pianist."

"Pianist?"

Grandpa looks at Marcolino and laughs. Then he says, "Let's check out the rockets."

The following Sunday Marcolino and his mom go to Grandpa's for lunch. Grandpa is a grand chef.

Grandpa puts lunch on the table, along with a box.
"What's this?" asks Marcolino.
"Something for your mom."

In the box are pictures of Mom when she was little.

THERE'S MOM ON HER BIKE . . .

. . . MOM AT KARATE CLASS

. . . MOM ON AN AIRPLANE RIDE

. . . MOM DRESSED AS A PIRATE

... MOM GARDENING

... MOM PERFORMING MAGIC

... MOM PAINTING

"You're missing a picture,"
Marcolino says.
"It must be lost," says Mom.

"Why are you making a face in this picture, Mom?" asks Marcolino.

"Your mom didn't like playing the piano," says Grandpa. "That's why she stopped taking lessons. Don't you remember, dear?"

Suddenly Mom's face turns red, as if a teacher were asking her why her homework wasn't done.

Now Marcolino knows the truth.
His mom didn't like playing the piano!
Mom and Grandpa send Marcolino into the living
room to finish his pie while they talk in the kitchen.

When they finish, Grandpa seems happy. It's
probably because he got an extra slice of pie.

The next day Grandpa takes
Marcolino to a music store.
"Marcolino, there are lots
of instruments. Pick out one
you like."

Now . . .

. . . every day at 3:00 sharp,
Marcolino practices his scales.

Poo Poo Poo Poo

Every day at 3:13, his mom asks,
"Aren't you tired? Would you like to
stop for a snack?"

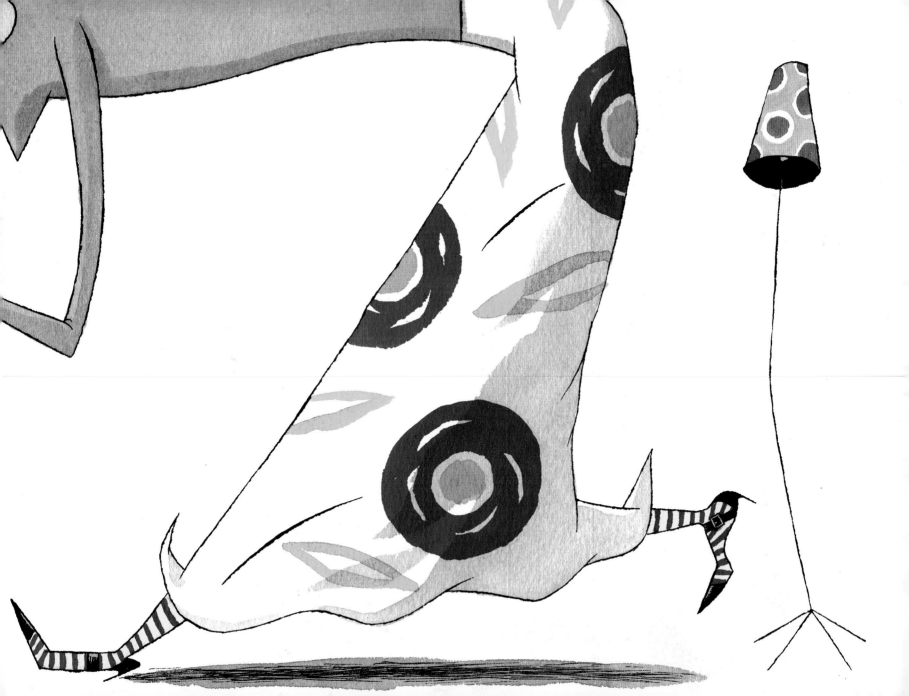

But Marcolino isn't tired, and he doesn't want
to stop for a snack.

He needs to practice to become . . .

. . . A GRAND TUBA PLAYER.

2007 First U.S. edition

Published by Charlesbridge
85 Main Street
Watertown, MA 02472
(617) 926-0329
www.charlesbridge.com

First published in France in 2005 by Éditions Sarbacane, 35 rue d'Hauteville,
75010 Paris, France, as *Piano Piano*. Copyright © 2005 by Éditions Sarbacane.

Library of Congress Cataloging-in-Publication Data
Cali, Davide.
     Piano, piano / Davide Cali ; illustrated by Éric Heliot ; [translated by
Randi Rivers].
          p. cm.
     Originally published: Paris : Éditions Sarbacane, 2005.
     Summary: Marcolino hates practicing his scales on the piano, but feels
he must because he is the reason his mother never became a grand pianist–
until his grandfather lets them both in on a little secret.
     ISBN 978-1-58089-191-2 (reinforced for library use)
[1. Piano–Instruction and study–Fiction. 2. Mothers and sons–Fiction.
3. Grandfathers–Fiction.] I. Heliot, Éric, ill. II. Rivers, Randi. III. Title.
PZ7.C1283Pia 2007
[E]–dc22   2006030241

Printed in China
(hc) 10 9 8 7 6 5 4 3 2 1

Text type set in Minya Nouvelle
Color separations by Chroma Graphics, Singapore
Printed and bound by Jade Productions
Production supervision by Brian G. Walker